ERASER

By **Anna Kang**

Illustrated by

Christopher Weyant

two lions

To Kelsey Skea,
editor extraordinaire and friend.
—A.K. & C.W.

Text copyright © 2018 by Anna Kang
Illustration copyright © 2018 by Christopher Weyant
All rights reserved.

Published by Two Lions, New York   www.apub.com
Amazon, the Amazon logo, and Two Lions are trademarks of Amazon.com, Inc., or its affiliates.
ISBN-13: 9781503902589   ISBN-10: 1503902587
The illustrations are rendered in ink and watercolor with brush pens on Arches paper.
Book design by Abby Dening   Printed in China   First Edition
2 4 6 8 10 9 7 5 3 1

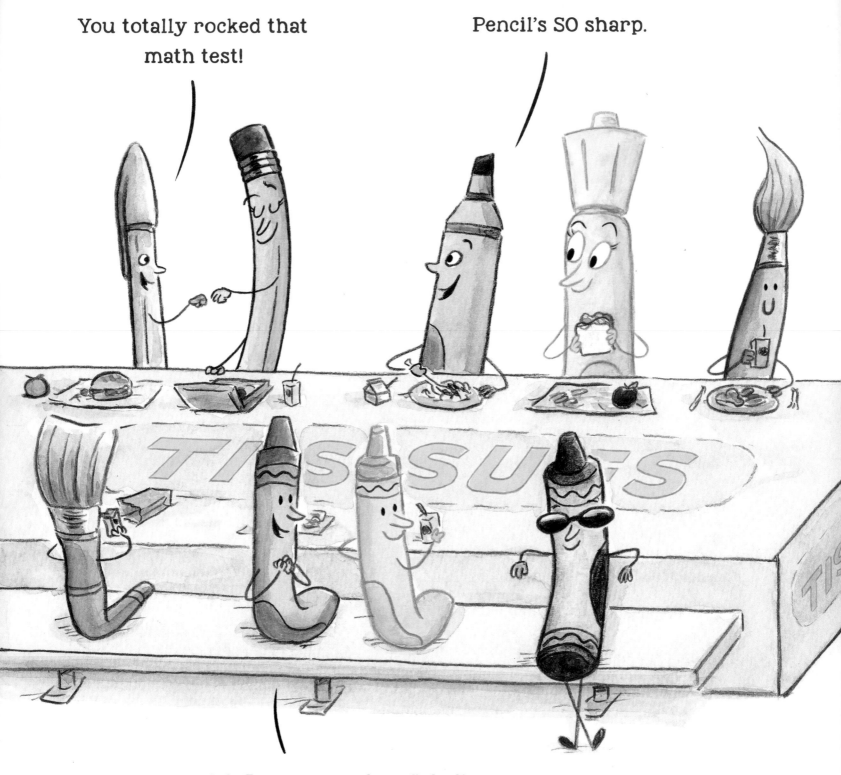

Everyone thinks Pencil and her friends
are the smart and creative ones.

It's not fair.

And look at Tape and Glue.
They can get anyone to stick together.
Even pipe cleaners and buttons.

KUMBAYAAA...

We all LOVE Paper.

Whenever I see you, I feel like I can do *anything*!

And Scissors—
well, she's just kind of scary.

I don't
run.
EVER.

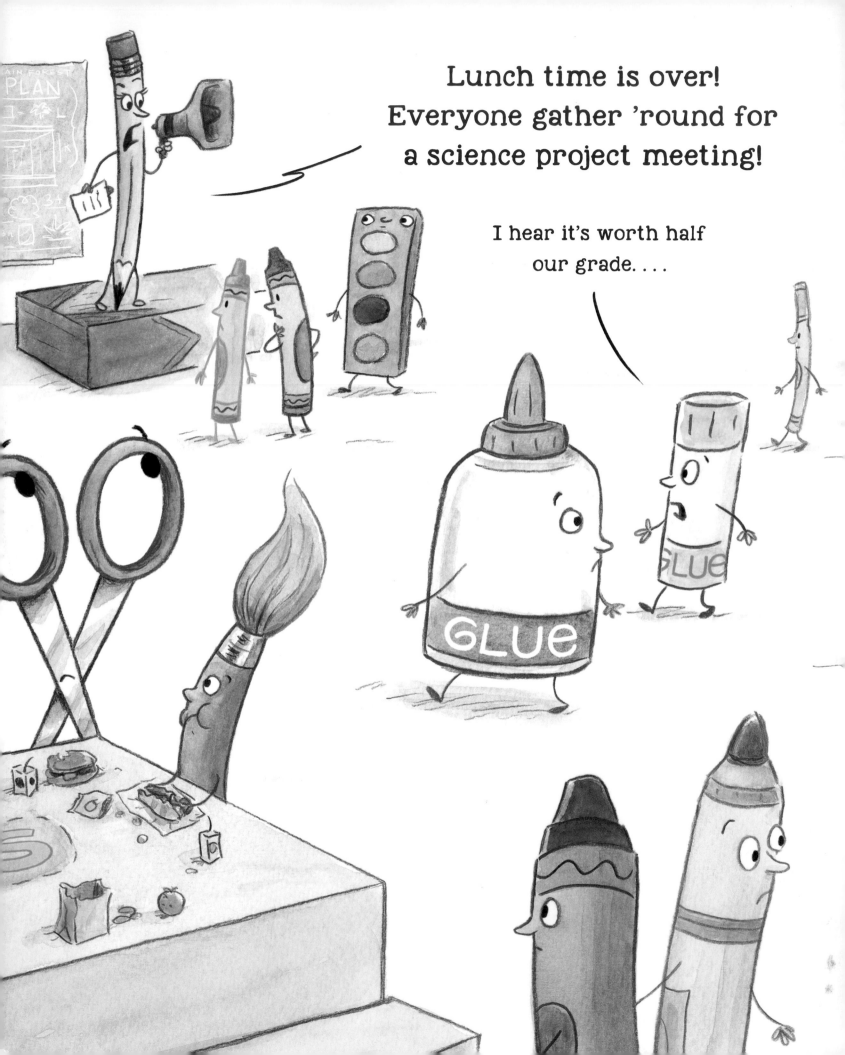

Not *you*, Eraser.
This is a *creative* meeting.

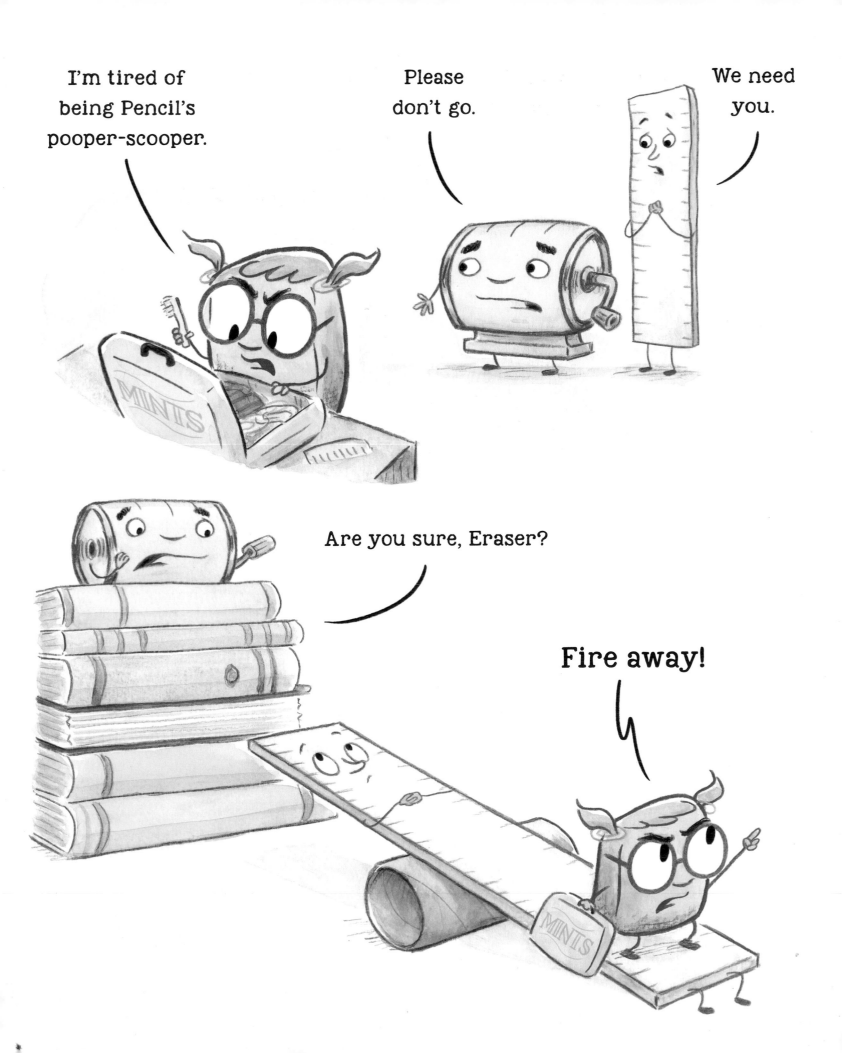

I LOVE your work.

I'm a huge fan.

You do?

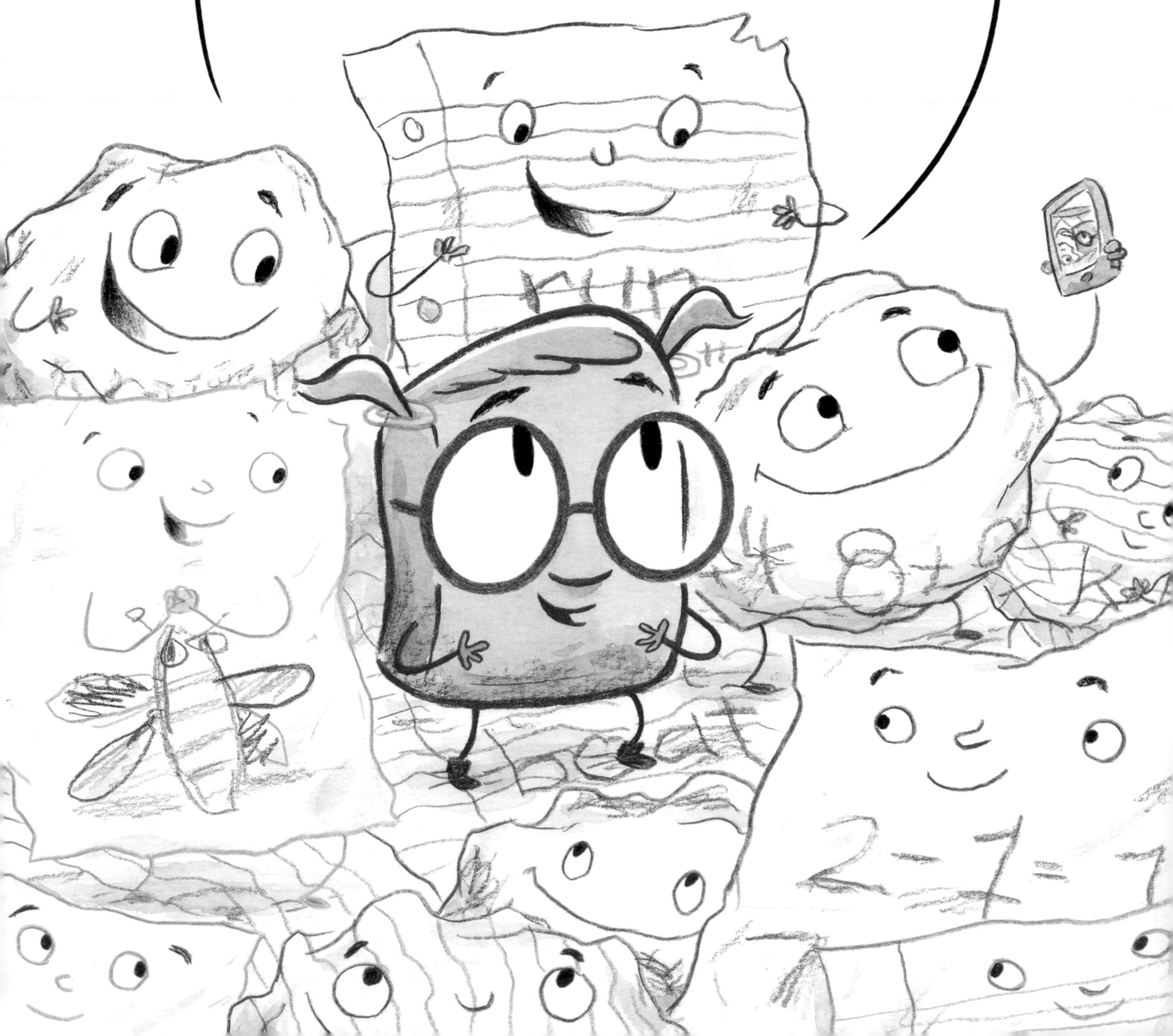

I DO create.
I create second chances.

Take your time. You're doing great.
We can always fix it. . . .